Dick
King~Smith

A BANANA BOOK

YOB

Dick King-Smith

Illustrated by
Abigail Pizer

MAMMOTH

First published in Great Britain 1986
by William Heinemann Ltd
Published 1995 by Mammoth
an imprint of Reed Consumer Books Ltd
Michelin House, 81 Fulham Road, London SW3 6RB
and Auckland, Melbourne, Singapore and Toronto

Text copyright © Dick King-Smith 1986
Illustrations copyright © Abigail Pizer 1986

ISBN 0 7497 2336 X

A CIP catalogue record for this title
is available from the British Library

Printed in Italy by Olivotto

'THERE'S A BODY!' yelled Joanna
suddenly. 'By the side of the road –
just back there – oh, stop, Dad, do!'

Her father did as he was told. He
stuck his head out of the window of
the Land-Rover and peered back
through the teeming rain that was
driving in across the moors from the
sea.

1

'Sheep, I expect, Jo,' he said. 'Got hit by a car, probably. They lose a lot like that in this part of the world.'

'It didn't look woolly,' Joanna said. 'It might have been a person.' She shivered. 'Oh please, Dad, let's go back and see.'

'All right, chicken, don't get yourself in a state,' said her father. He put the Land-Rover in reverse. 'Like I said, it'll be an old sheep. Tell me when to stop, I can't see a thing in all this rain.'

'Bit further,' said Joanna, head stuck through the side-window.

'Bit further. Stop! Oh, Dad!'

'What is it?'

'It's a dog!'

'Dead?'

'I don't know. It's not moving. Oh, Dad, please have a look.'

Her father sighed and got out. He walked around the back of the Land-Rover and bent, hands on knees, to look at the large limp shape that lay, with the raindrops bouncing off it, at the edge of the moorland road.

'Dead as a button, I should think,' he shouted above the noise of the storm. 'Great big chap too – whoever hit him will have a good old dent in their car, I should think.'

'Is there a name and address on his collar?'

'Half a tick. No address, just his name. ''Boy''. Poor old Boy. Not much we can do for him, I'm afraid.'

But when Joanna's father got back into the Land-Rover one look at his

daughter's face told him all he needed to know. Mr Best was a farmer and well used to dealing with all kinds of awkward animals – high-spirited horses, cross-grained pigs and hot-eyed bulls. But always, when he saw his eight-year-old daughter's chin set firm and her eyes blaze, he knew that there was more trouble ahead than he could handle.

'There's nothing we can do, Jo,' he said again. 'We'd better get on. We've had a long day at the Show and we've got a long way to go yet before we're home.'

'We can't . . . just . . . leave him here.'

'But look, chicken, we haven't even any idea who he belongs to.'

'Dad!'

A couple of hours later the Land-

Rover turned off a main road, down a lane, and into the yard of the Bests' farm. Joanna's mother came out to greet them.

'Did you have a good day at the Show?' she said. 'What was the weather like?'

'Show was all right,' said her husband. 'As for the weather, it was enough to make a parson swear. It rained cats and . . . it was very wet.'

'Jo? Have you had a nice time?'

'We found a dog,' said Joanna in a voice of deepest gloom, 'that had been run over. He's called Boy . . . he was called Boy. He's in the back. Dad has promised to bury him . . . in the orchard . . . under the pear-tree. I'm going to make a cross and put his name on it,' and she stumped off, head bowed in mourning.

Mr Best let down the tail-gate of the Land-Rover.

'Look at the thing,' he said to his wife. 'It's the size of a month-old Friesian calf.'

'Couldn't you have just left it?'

'She wouldn't let me,' said her husband.

He took hold of the hindlegs to pull the body out.

'Funny,' he said. 'He still feels quite warm,' and then they saw, in the clear sunlight of a now fine evening, the gentle rise and fall of the dog's ribs.

'Jo!' shouted Mr Best. 'Jo!' and as she came running back, 'Look!'

Slowly, as though waking from a deep sleep, the dog called Boy opened his eyes.

'Well, there's nothing terribly serious wrong with him,' said the vet.

It was later that evening, and the dog had undergone a thorough examination. He had submitted to it without protest, perhaps realising, as animals do, that someone was trying to help him. He did not wag his tail but simply stood quite still with a faraway look in his eyes.

'He doesn't answer to his name,'

said Mr Best. 'Boy! Boy! See, he
doesn't even look at me.'

'Shock, I expect,' said the vet. 'He's
obviously been concussed. No bones
broken, but he's had one heck of a

bang on the head. Has he eaten anything?'

'No. We've offered him food, but it was funny, he sat and looked at it but he wouldn't touch it, almost as though we'd told him not to.'

'I'm sure he wanted it,' Joanna said. 'He was dribbling.'

'Oh well,' said the vet, 'he'll eat when he's hungry enough. A good night's sleep won't do him any harm. He seems to have had quite a day what with being knocked out cold in the middle of Exmoor in a storm, and then coming to and finding himself in a strange place with strange people. He's a fine big fellow, isn't he?'

'What sort of a dog is he, d'you think?' Joanna asked.

'Well, he's not pure bred, that's for sure. If you're asking me for an educated guess I should say he's Irish Wolfhound cross Labrador. Got his size from his father and that black satiny coat from his mum. No chance of entering him in Shows and adding to all those silver cups your father's won for his cattle. But then you'll try to find his owners, I imagine?'

'I've already contacted the police,' said Mr Best.

'What if they can't trace them?'

'Well I suppose we'll have to find him a good home.'

'He's got a good home,' said Joanna very quietly.

'Now look, chicken . . .'

'Dad!'

'We'll see.'

'Well now, I must be off,' said the vet. 'Let me know how he goes on.' He patted the dog's back. 'Finished with you, old chap. You can take the weight off your feet. Sit!' The dog remained standing. The only movement he made was to turn his head and look at the vet with what Joanna thought was a puzzled expression.

'Sit!' said the vet again, with no result.

'Funny,' said Mr Best. 'You'd have thought he'd have been trained to do that at least. After all, he's not a puppy.'

'No,' said the vet, picking up his bag and turning to leave the room, 'I should say he's at least two years old. Why he doesn't know a simple command like that I simply cannot under*stand.*'

At the sound of the last part of this final word the dog immediately sat down. Only Joanna saw this, for the two men had walked out.

'You funny old Boy,' she said. 'Now at last you've decided to sit.' No sooner had she spoken that last word than the dog stood up again, looking

at her to see if he had done the right thing. But when without thinking she said 'Good dog,' he looked distinctly unhappy. He hung his head and his long tail went between his legs.

'What's the matter?' said Joanna. 'There's no need to look so miserable. You haven't done anything bad.'

Once again this final word produced a very odd result. Up came Boy's head and out came his tail and began to wag, slowly. A ridiculous idea suddenly occurred to Joanna. 'He's had

one heck of a bang on the head,' the vet had said. Bangs on the head did funny things to people, didn't they? Might not bangs on the head do funny things to dogs?

Just suppose, she thought . . . could it possibly be that . . . well, there's only one way to find out.

'Bad,' she said again, softly.

The tail wagged faster.

'Bad,' said Joanna in a louder voice. 'Bad! Bad!! You *bad* dog!!' and the big black animal wagged his tail like mad and whined with pleasure and licked her hand.

The truth burst upon Joanna.

'Stand!' she commanded, and Boy sat.

'Sit!' she ordered, and he stood up again.

'*Bad dog!*' said Joanna severely, and

a moment after that her father came back into the room to see his daughter kneeling with her arms round the dog's neck, having her face thoroughly washed, while Boy's whole body curved to and fro in an ecstasy of tail-wagging.

'Oh, Dad!' cried Joanna. 'I've found out what's wrong . . . he's got everything back to front in his mind

. . . it must have been that bang on the head . . . just watch!'

She got to her feet.

'Stand!' she told Boy and he sat down.

She ran to the door.

'Come!' she called and he stayed exactly where he was.

Then she ran out of the room, and came back with a big bowl of food.

She put it on the floor at the far side of the room as man and dog looked on. They both stayed quite still, but one began to dribble.

'Now then, Dad,' said Joanna, 'watch this,' and she turned to the dog.

'Stay!' she said and he came to her.

'Sit,' she said and he stood beside her.

She pointed at the bowl.

'Eat it up!' she said.

Still he stood, looking up at her, waiting for the next command. Joanna grinned at her father.

'Now then,' she said to Boy, 'don't you touch that food, d'you hear me? Don't you dare touch it,' and before the words were out of her mouth the meat was in his, as he gulped and swallowed, gulped and swallowed, and finally polished the bowl with his tongue.

'So that's why he wouldn't eat before!' said Mr Best, softly. 'Because we kept telling him "Eat it up, eat it up, there's a good dog".'

'Which means "Don't touch that, you bad dog" now,' said Joanna. 'Everything's opposite.'

'Only one thing I don't understand, chicken,' said her father. 'Why won't he answer to his name? Boy! Boy! See, he doesn't even look at me.'

'Like I told you, Dad,' said Joanna. 'Everything's opposite now. You're still calling him by his old name, the

name he answered to before his accident. We can't use that any more.'

She went to the door and she called 'Yob! Stay!'

And Yob came running.

Next morning Mr Best sat stirring his tea. His wife was washing up, his daughter had gone to the village school, and, with a couple of hours of the day's work already done, he felt like sitting quietly with his third cup and thinking. Usually he thought about problems, like a sick cow or a broken-down tractor or if it would rain (when he wanted it to) or keep dry (when he wanted it to). Now he was thinking about Yob.

'Stay,' he said, and the dog came. 'Up, Yob!'

With a grunt of relief the dog settled at his feet.

'Finished your tea, Bill?' asked Mrs Best, coming in.

'Mm. I was just thinking.'

'About the dog? Whether to keep him?'

'Jo's very keen to.'

'Well then that's that,' said his wife, with a smile. 'And anyway he's a lovely . . .'

'Careful!'

'I mean, he's a horrible nasty bad dog!'

Yob's tail thumped happily.

'And I suppose,' she said, 'we'll all get used to doing everything backwards.' She took an uneaten slice of toast from the rack and dropped it in front of Yob's nose.

'Don't touch!' she said, and he ate it.

'What's worrying me, Mary,' said her husband, 'is that he's very likely to be claimed. A dog like that . . . been well-fed . . . name on his collar . . . been trained even if he's got it all scrambled now . . . someone's bound to be looking for him. They'll take him back and that's going to break Jo's heart.'

At that moment the phone rang.

'A chap's coming about four o'clock,' said Mr Best after he'd replaced the receiver.

'Oh dear. Jo will be home from school by then.'

'What's the matter?' said Joanna when she saw her parents' gloomy faces. 'It's not Yob? He's not ill?'

'No,' said her father, 'but he's been traced, Jo. A man's coming to collect him, shortly.'

'Oh,' said Joanna.

'Look, chicken, we'll get you a puppy. You're old enough for a dog of your own.'

'I don't want a puppy,' said Joanna. 'I just want Yob.'

Yob's tail banged the floor at the

sound of his name and then came
another sound, of a car. There was a
knock on the front door.

Half of Joanna wanted to rush away
so as not to set eyes on this person,
not to see him take the dog away, not
to have to say goodbye. The other
half, the curious half, made her hide
behind the curtains.

Peeping round, she saw her parents
showing a man into the room, a short
fat man with a very red face.

'Ah, there you are, Boy,' he said in

a loud voice. 'Boy! Boy?'

Yob, who was sitting on the hearth-rug, did not even look round.

'He doesn't seem to know you,' said Mr Best. 'Have you had him since he was a puppy?'

'No. I bought him quite recently from people going abroad. I wanted a big animal – as a guard dog, you know. I've a great many valuable things in my house.'

Bet you haven't got masses of silver cups like Dad has, thought Joanna behind the curtains, and you look horrid and you sound horrid and I wish I hadn't stayed to see you.

'Of course we've only been looking after him for twenty-four hours,' said Mr Best, 'but we find he doesn't always do exactly as he's told.'

'He'll do as I tell him,' said the

red-faced man. 'Get up, Boy!' Yob lay down.

'Come!' said the man in an even louder voice.

The dog stayed put.

'What the devil's the matter with him?' said the red-faced man.

Mr Best caught his wife's eye and then said, 'Do what you're told, there's a good dog.'

At these last words Yob looked the picture of misery.

'Did I understand you to say,' said the red-faced man slowly, 'that he'd had a bang on the head?'

'A heck of a bang.'

'He doesn't look well to me.'

'No, he doesn't, does he?'

'Something very wrong with him.'

'So it seems.'

'Well see here, Mr Best, I don't

believe in beating about the bush. A dog that behaves as strangely as that is no use to me.' Behind the red-faced man the curtains moved a fraction.

'He's not a bit of good to me,' he went on (and at 'good' Yob cringed even further away), 'so you do what you like with him. Waste of my time coming all this way. I'll be off.'

'Jo! Jo! Where are you?' called her father when the man had gone.

'Here,' said Joanna, coming out, 'and you said I was old enough for a dog of my own.'

As time passed, the Bests grew used to living with an animal to whom 'Yes' meant 'No'.

Sometimes indeed they fell into the same way of thinking themselves, and for example a breakfast-time conversation might run like this:

Mr B: Don't pass the marmalade, Jo.

Joanna (passing it): Shan't.

Mrs B (absently): Don't speak so *politely* to your father.

Mr B: When I said 'marmalade', I meant 'honey'.

Joanna: Can I get up? I've started.

Mrs B: Of course not. (Joanna gets down.)

But on the whole they reserved back-to-front language for the dog Yob. There were two things they learned not to say in his hearing. One

was 'Be quiet', which made him bark
like mad, and the other was 'Down!'

Yob's response to this word was to
leap up and, standing on his hindlegs,
place his forefeet on the speaker's
shoulders (luckily they were Mr
Best's), and attempt to lick him to
death.

'He really is the friendliest dog,
isn't he, Bill?' said Mrs Best, one day
when they'd had Yob for a while.

'Yes. Fat lot of use he'd have been to that chap as a guard dog.'

'I suppose he might have been fierce before his accident changed things. D'you suppose he was running away from home when he got hit?'

'I bet he was,' said Joanna. 'I bet he was trying to find his first owners. Trying to get away from that man. I didn't like him one bit. Horrible beast!' and at these last words Yob came to her squirming with pleasure.

'What d'you suppose he'd do to a burglar, Dad?' she said.

'Kiss him.'

A couple of weeks later, a burglar came.

Burglars come in all shapes and sizes, and this one was small and thin and always posed as a businessman. He would stay at a country hotel or

pub and liked to chat with the locals.
He was interested in old houses, he
told them. Were there any stately
homes in the district? Or Georgian
mansions? Or Queen Anne manor-
houses? Or even an Elizabethan
farmhouse? Thus he learned that the
Bests lived in such a house, and that
Bill Best had won many valuable silver
cups and trophies with his pedigree
dairy cows.

Well worth melting down, thought the burglar, and next day he drove straight to the Bests' farm and knocked on the door.

'I'm sorry to trouble you,' he said to Mrs Best when she opened it, 'but I've lost my way. I wonder if you could direct me to . . . ', and he gave the name of a village a few miles away.

While she was talking, he noted (with pleasure) that the catch on the nearest window was a simple one to force and (with annoyance) that there

was a very large black dog standing in the hall.

'What a big fellow!' he said. 'Is he friendly?'

Mrs Best laughed.

'My husband thinks,' she said, 'that if a burglar came, Yob would probably give him a kiss!'

That afternoon the burglar bought something in a butcher's shop. That evening he parked his car in an out-of-the-way spot not far from the farm, and prepared for action.

When the grandfather clock in the hall struck twelve for midnight (a noise through which the family, as always, slept, but which covered the

sound of a carefully opened window),
a figure slipped over the sill and stood
listening.

The burglar was wearing a black
track-suit. On his feet were black
plimsolls, on his hands black leather
gloves. Over his eyes was a black
mask. In his left hand was a sack, in
his right hand a torch. In his pocket
was a pound of fresh pig's liver. In the
liver was a powerful sleeping-pill.

Just my luck, thought the burglar

happily, as a great array of silver cups
and silver bowls and even a silver
model of a cow winked and sparkled at
him in the beam of his torch.

At that moment there was a noise
in the next room that sounded like a
yawn, which it was.

Just my luck, thought the burglar
sadly, as the torchlight shone on the
large black figure standing in the
connecting doorway.

'Hullo, Yob,' he said very softly.

Yob wagged gently at the sound of his name.

Dropping the sack, the burglar drew the lump of meat from his pocket and tossed it on the floor. The delicious smell of the pig's liver filled Yob's nostrils, and he stood and stared at this nice man, hoping for the right command.

'Eat it up,' whispered the burglar.

Yob stood, waiting.

'Eat it up,' whispered the burglar again. 'Eat it up, there's a good boy!'

At these words Yob backed unhappily away, banged into a small table, and tipped it over.

'Be quiet!' hissed the burglar, and at this Yob began to bark.

'Stop it!' said the burglar, so Yob kept on, loudly enough now to wake the dead, let alone the Bests.

'You *horrible* dog!' the burglar snarled. 'Why don't you pipe *down*!'

When Mr Best appeared, shotgun in hand, and turned on the lights, he saw before him on the floor a lump of raw meat.

Beyond that lay Yob, and under Yob lay a black-clad figure that struggled feebly under a shower of kisses which increased to a slobbery storm as the burglar cried, 'Oh stop it, stop it, you beastly dog!'

When the police had come and taken the burglar away, the Bests looked fondly at Yob.

'Isn't he wicked!' said Joanna.

'Dreadful!' said her mother.

Her father looked at the congealing liver.

'I think you deserve a big reward,' he said to Yob, 'but that will do for a start. Don't touch it!'

They watched as the hero of the night gulped it down. Then suddenly his eyes began to glaze and his legs to buckle, until finally, like a great tree falling, he crashed to the floor and lay still.

'That meat was laced with dope,' said the vet later. 'He'll be out cold for a while. Last time I saw him I seem to remember saying that a good night's sleep wouldn't do him any harm. That's what he's going to get.'

'We could all do with some,' said Mr Best. 'Go on, chicken, up you go.'

Joanna tried hard to stay awake but suddenly, it seemed, it was broad daylight. She jumped out of bed and rushed downstairs. Yob still lay exactly as he had fallen. For an instant he looked as dead as when first she had set eyes on him, but then she heard him snoring. Joanna sat on the floor beside him.

There's only one way to wake you, she thought, and she lifted the flap of his ear.

'Go to sleep!' she said.

Contrary as ever, the dog opened his eyes.

'Bad-morning, Yob!' said Joanna happily.

There are lots of Bananas for you to enjoy!

THE ERL KING'S DAUGHTER - Joan Aiken
THE QUEST OF THE GOLDEN DRAGON
- June Counsel
IMP - Marjorie Darke
SCAREDY-CAT - Anne Fine
THE MOON MONSTERS - Douglas Hill
HOW JENNIFER (AND SPECKLE) SAVED THE
EARTH - Douglas Hill
BEWARE, PRINCESS! - Mary Hoffman
DRACULA'S DAUGHTER - Mary Hoffman
WHO'S A CLEVER GIRL, THEN? - Rose Impey
CROCODILE DOG - Gene Kemp
THE BIG STINK - Sheila Lavelle
THE DISAPPEARING GRANNY - Sheila Lavelle
DEBBIE AND THE THE LITTLE DEVIL
- Penelope Lively
DRAGON TROUBLE - Penelope Lively
SASHA AND THE BICYLE THIEVES - Errol Lloyd
CONKER - Michael Morpurgo
JANE AND THE PIRATES - Jules Older
NO GUNS, NO ORANGES - Ann Pilling
THE PHANTOM CARWASH - Chris Powling
LIGHTNING FRED - Dick King-Smith
YOB - Dick King-Smith
THE GHOST CHILD - Emma Tennant